AF281692

Sandra Hohmann

UNSEEN

Performance with music

FSC
www.fsc.org
MIX
Papier aus ver-
antwortungsvollen
Quellen
Paper from
responsible sources
FSC® C105338

Bibliografische Information der Deutschen
Nationalbibliothek:
Die Deutsche Nationalbibliothek verzeichnet diese
Publikation in der Deutschen Nationalbibliografie;
detaillierte bibliografische Daten sind im Internet über
http://dnb.dnb.de abrufbar.

© 2019 2022 2023 Sandra Hohmann

Herstellung und Verlag: BoD – Books on Demand, Norderstedt

ISBN: 978-3-7568-6050-0

To all the children
that have gone missing.

Someone will always care.

CONTENTS

PREFACE

Children go missing all the time. Every year, every month, every week, every day. Most of them are, luckily, un-missed rather quickly. They played hide and seek, they got lost on their way or they deliberately ran away and come back or are brought back. Or they have been taken against their will but can escape or are released – by someone they knew or by a stranger.

Still, thousands and thousands of children don't come back. They remain missing, for days, months, years, for more than a lifetime. They are not seen again. As if they had just vanished into thin air, though they were often taken in plain sight. A reminder that people too often don't see what they don't want to see.

Someone knows what has happened to these children. Who has happened to them.

But only because I don't know what has happened doesn't mean that I will forget.

CHARACTERS

JESSICA (GIRL) (7 to 8 YEARS, FEMALE)

RATHER LONG HAIR, IN THE BEGINNING BRAIDED, WEARS A DRESS in SCENES 1 to 3, AFTER THAT A NIGHTGOWN. DOESN'T SPEAK OR MAKE ANY NOISES THROUGHOUT THE ENTIRE PLAY

JESSICA (WOMAN) (AROUND 20 YEARS, FEMALE)

SLIGHTLY RESEMBLING "JESSICA (GIRL)", RATHER THIN, RUGGED APPEARANCE, FACE APPEARS EMOTIONLESS.

SHADOW

COMPARABLE TO THE SHADOW IN "M – EINE STADT SUCHT EINEN MÖRDER", A HUGE SHADOW, MAYBE WEARING A HAT OR A COAT; SOMEHOW "MALE" APPEARANCE.

VOICES (MALE AND FEMALE, MAINLY ADULTS)

MASKED PEOPLE

Persons in SCENE 5 who do not look like actual persons, but like the articles, etc. they are carrying in their hands.

Scene One

Empty stage. DARKNESS.

In the middle, not really recognizable without lights, JESSICA (GIRL) is sitting on the floor, clutching her arms around her angled legs, her head resting on her knees.

After a few seconds, very little light is turned on, modest spot on JESSICA (GIRL) in the middle.

Then VOICES from the OFF start yelling (see below), at the same time headlines of newspaper articles, screenshots / short videos of TV news, etc. (see below) are projected onto the stage. Both the yelling and the projection of headlines accelerate for about 30 seconds, starting with a single hesitant yelling and a single headline that is projected for 2 or 3 seconds and ending in frenzy.

Yelling:

"Jessica?"

"Where are you?"

"Don't hide, Jessica!"

"It's not funny anymore, where are you?"

"Come back, Jessica!"

"Please come home, sweetie."

"I miss you, please come back."

"Please bring back our daughter!"

"What have you done to her?"

"Why her? Why?"

PROJECTION of headlines:

"Girl (7) missing since May 2nd"

"Jessica was on her way to school"

"Where is Jessica?"

"Jessica's parents in despair"

"What happened to the little girl?"

"Jessica is still missing – no trace yet"

"Missing for over a month – Is there still hope?"

"Debbie and Thomas won't give up on their daughter"

"Will we ever find out what happened"

"Two years ago: Jessica vanished"

PROJECTION of TV news:

Female reporter in the studio: "The police is asking for help: Who has seen 7-year-old Jessica? She was last seen ..."

Male reporter in front of a house / on the sidewalk: "Jessica vanished on her way to school, no one seems to have seen the little girl after she has left her home right here", and he points to the house behind him.

VOICES go silent, projection ends.

MUSIC starts: Black Sabbath – Snowblind.

Snow starts falling.

MUSIC fades out at 2:19 min.

SUDDEN DARKNESS.

SCENE TWO

Interior of a bright ground floor apartment, kitchen.

In the middle a kitchen table with a Tupper box and a juice box on it. On the kitchen counter is a stuffed mouse.

At the back of the stage a window, a sunny day outside, a street that leads straight away from the kitchen window, houses along the street.

A calendar on the wall shows May 2nd.

MUSIC starts: Johnossi - Man must dance.

Kitchen door opens, JESSICA (GIRL) comes in with a satchel in her hands.

She puts the satchel down to the floor and is more jumping to the music than walking, smiling, overjoyed.

JESSICA (GIRL) jumps/dances around the table, finally grabs the Tupper box and the juice box and puts both into her satchel.

JESSICA (GIRL) dances over to the stuffed mouse, takes it, cuddles it, and puts it into her satchel as well, leaves the kitchen and closes the door behind her.

MUSIC fades out at 2:17 min.

SCENE THREE

Still interior of the apartment.

MUSIC starts: Portugal.The Man — Shade (complete song).

JESSICA (GIRL) can be seen through the kitchen window, waves goodbye to someone, smiles, turns around and walks down the street. Turns around again while walking, still smiling, waves again.

JESSICA (GIRL) continues walking, looks to the left, to the right, up to the sky, curiously, joyfully.

JESSICA (GIRL) is finally in the far, small at the horizon.

SHORT DARKNESS.

SCENE FOUR

In the street, the street leading from right to left now.

MUSIC starts: Belasco – The Hunters song.

JESSICA (GIRL) walking onto the stage from the right, smiling, maybe whistling to the song, waving her head to the melody, the rhythm.

SHADOW approaches JESSICA (GIRL) from the front of the stage.

JESSICA (GIRL) turns to SHADOW at 0:47 min of the song ("so, when you see that monster, don't run away").

JESSICA (GIRL) looks up to SHADOW, smiles at him as if she has found a treasure.

JESSICA (GIRL) reaches her hand out to SHADOW. At 0:58 min of the song ("Take it easy"), SHADOW takes JESSICA (GIRL) by the hand and they both continue to walk down the street, to the left of the stage.

JESSICA (GIRL) and SHADOW have left the stage before the last "You'll be home someday" can be heard.

SCENE FIVE

A cellar / lower floor, small room, no apparent
windows, grey concrete walls, the audience will
look down on it, together with SHADOW, the
perpetrator, through a small window in a steel
door that can be opened by sliding (just as the
mechanism on massive doors in a jail or
psychiatric institution, but there's also a
window glass that reflects the eyes of the
person looking through it). The eyes of SHADOW
will be reflected in the glass window of the
door, so that the audience will both see the
reflection of the eyes and look into the room
from SHADOW'S perspective.

JESSICA (GIRL) is in the room, yet everything
is dark at the beginning of the scene.

During the whole scene, several MASKED PEOPLE
walk onto the stage and put the newspaper
articles, posters, etc. that were used in SCENE
1 onto the outer walls of the room.

At the beginning of the scene, the slide of the
window in the door is opened abruptly and with
a terrifyingly loud BANG, and immediately
starts

MUSIC: Antiseen - Psycho Killer (complete
song).

JESSICA (GIRL) starts to jump and dance
frantically to the music, and she mouths the

refrain "Psycho Killer - Qu'est-que c'est?".
During the lines "Run run run run" she runs
towards the concrete walls, stops at first, but
running faster and more determined as the song
progresses and finally (at about 2:13 min of
the song) violently hits the walls. From then
on, cages come down on the girl, they are
getting smaller and smaller, JESSICA (GIRL) is
moving and hitting the bars until the last cage
is finally so small that JESSICA (GIRL) can't
move anymore.

The audience can see SHADOW laughing towards
the end of the song (along with the singer from
ca. 2:54 min onwards).

MUSIC ends and the slide of the window is shut
again with a loud BANG.

Scene Six

It is night, moon and stars shine above the stage, and there's a dim, but warm light on JESSICA (GIRL) and immediately at the beginning of the scene starts

MUSIC: Johannes Brahms - Wiegenlied. (Spieluhr-Version von "Spieluhrträume")

The stars are sparkling, it looks like stars and blossoms are raining down, it's a fairy tale scene.

The song plays until ca. 1:32 min, then immediately starts the MUSIC of SCENE SEVEN.

SCENE SEVEN

The stage is dark, MUSIC starts:

Nine Inch Nails - Closer (Precursor)

Shady lights, flickering.

SHADOW is sneaking and creeping around the cellar room, only his shadow is visible on the outer walls. From 1:56 min on, his steps are in synchronicity with the music.

At ca. 2:17 min the MUSIC fades out and SHADOW leaves the stage.

SCENE EIGHT

Stage similar to SCENE SIX, calm night.

MUSIC starts: Rundfunk-Jugendchor Wernigerode - Stille Nacht, heilige Nacht

The song plays until 0:55 min, then immediately starts the MUSIC of SCENE NINE.

SCENE NINE

Dark stage, immediately starts

MUSIC: Nine Inch Nails – Closer (Precursor) at 4:35 min ("I wanna fuck you like an animal") until ca. 4:46 min and then 4:38 min until ca. 4:46 min ("like an animal") in a loop for about one minute.

At the beginning of the scene, SHADOW sneaks around JESSICA (GIRL), who is still in the cages, from a distance, but he gets closer and closer and with the last "animal" he has reached her, and the stage goes dark.

<h1 align="center">SCENE TEN</h1>

Stage resembles that of SCENE SIX and SCENE EIGHT, but the light isn't warm anymore, the stars are not sparkling, the fairy tale scene has obvious cracks.

MUSIC starts: Lisa Wahlandt - Müde bin ich, geh zur Ruh (until 0:20 min in a loop for 6 times).

SCENE ELEVEN

Dark stage, immediately starts

MUSIC: Marilyn Manson – Dance of the Dope Hats (Remix) until 0:49 min and the last seconds before 0:49 min in a loop for several times.

Together with the MUSIC, projections start. Like strobe light, single images are projected onto the walls only for the blink of an eye, showing the torture and molestation of JESSICA (GIRL).

The scene ends with a loud BANG and a sudden DARK STAGE.

Scene Twelve

The stage is covered in cold light, everything appears PALE, COLD, FROZEN, LIFELESS.

As soon as this cold light is switched on, MUSIC starts: OMD – Joan of Arc (until 0:35 min).

Scene Thirteen

JESSICA (GIRL) is crouching in the smallest cage in a cage in a cage.

MUSIC starts: Tocotronic - Explosion

As the song progresses, the newspaper articles, etc. that had been put onto the walls throughout the former scenes are blown away in an enormous storm, as are sheets of the calendar, marking the progression of time.

As the song ends, the stage is empty except for the crouching GIRL in the cages.

SCENE FOURTEEN

JESSICA (GIRL) has turned into JESSICA (WOMAN) that is crouching in the same position as JESSICA (GIRL) did in the last scene.

The stage is dark except for a spot on JESSICA (WOMAN) in the cages.

JESSICA (WOMAN) – at this point not apparent to the audience – doesn't wear clothes.

MUSIC starts: Arcade Fire – My body is a cage.

The cages slowly, one after another, disappear, while JESSICA (WOMAN) does not change her position until all cages have disappeared at 2:00 min of the song. Then JESSICA (WOMAN) slowly stands up and we can see that on her bare skin, all over her body, are the bars of a cage. JESSICA (WOMAN) stands on the stage, with empty eyes staring into oblivion.

The part of the SONG from 2:10 min to 2:24 min is repeated four times and fades out during the last repetition.

SCENE FIFTEEN

The stage is dark.

MUSIC starts: Joy Division - New Dawn Fades.

Photos of JESSICA (GIRL) are projected on the walls, in concordance with the rhythm of the music.

The first photo shows her right after birth and we can see JESSICA (GIRL) growing up happily on the following photos, the last one shows her right before she disappeared.

The projection stops in the moment before the singing would start, and while the song continues, spot on JESSICA (WOMAN) who is still standing in the middle of the stage as she was at the end of the last scene, with the bars of the cage on her body.

At 2:09 min of the song, the line "so you say" is repeated several times and the MUSIC fades out.

During the fade out, the stage suddenly goes dark again and immediately starts

MUSIC: Belasco - The Hunters song.

--- END ---

ABOUT **THIS TEXT** (2019)

This piece has been in the making for 5 years. It is an attempt to put children in the center – children that have vanished, that have been and still are molested or tortured. It is impossible to do them justice, but I do hope that this piece contributes just a little bit to remembering them.

ADDENDUM (2023)

Two things caught my attention when I read this text after a few years after I had first published it in 2019:

First, there's "Shadow". I am not sure I would name this person "Shadow" again – it was an attempt to be as far from being a certain "type", especially on the surface, as possible. But at the same time, it supports the old myth of "stranger danger". And that would be far from reality. Most children are harmed by people they grow up with.

And then there is the name "Jessica". I am not sure how I got to that name, but now I immediately thought of a girl who was named Jessica and died a horrible death after a more than horrible life at the age of 7 years. This happened 2005 in Hamburg, Germany.

I've dealt with this case a lot, contemplating how to tell such a story in a novel, and I am still trying to do this. It is likely that I had this case in the back of my mind when I started writing this performance.

MENTIONED MUSIC

In Order of Mentioning:

Black Sabbath - Snowblind

Johnossi - Man must dance

Portugal.The Man - Shade

Belasco - The Hunters song

Antiseen - Psycho Killer

Johannes Brahms - Wiegenlied (Music box version / Spieluhr-Version, sampler „Spieluhrträume")

Nine Inch Nails - Closer (Precursor)

Franz-Xaver Gruber / Joseph Mohr: Stille Nacht, heilige Nacht (performed by Rundfunk-Jugendchor Wernigerode)

Luise Hensel - Müde bin ich, geh zur Ruh (performed by Lisa Wahlandt

Marilyn Manson - Dance of the Dope Hats (Remix)

OMD - Joan of Arc

Tocotronic - Explosion

Arcade Fire - My body is a cage

Joy Division - New Dawn Fades